Poppy
and the Outdoors Cat

Poppy
and the Outdoors Cat

Dorothy Haas

Pictures by Margot Apple

ALBERT WHITMAN & COMPANY, CHICAGO

For Art
Who usually sees
the larger picture —
with humor

Library of Congress Cataloging in Publication Data

Haas, Dorothy.
  Poppy and the outdoors cat.

  SUMMARY: Because their house is too small for a
pet, Poppy Flower trains her newly-found cat to be an
"outdoors cat."
  [1. Cats — fiction] I. Apple, Margot. II. Title.
PZ7.H1124Po   [Fic]   80-19140
ISBN 0-8075-6621-7

Contents

1

Seven Children...Seven Pets?

"Not a great big dog," said Poppy. "Just a teeny one."

A book lay on the kitchen table next to her bowl. With a finger she traced the dog in the picture. He was leaning out of a car window, his long ears blowing in the wind, and he looked as though he was laughing. The corners of Poppy's mouth lifted. You just had to laugh back at that dog!

"No dog, Poppy," Mother said quietly. "We all step over each other as it is. A dog would only be underfoot."

"Oh, but it wouldn't," said Poppy. "I'd take care of it and play with it and feed it—"

"We don't exactly need another mouth to

feed," said Mother. But she smiled and sat down beside Poppy.

It was noontime in the Flowers' sunny old kitchen. The boys had already gone back to school, and the twins were playing out on the front-hall landing. Little Woody was happily busy under the table, dropping plastic spoons into a plastic milk bottle and shaking them out again. The kitchen smelled of chicken soup and the brownies cooling on the sink and the apples from the wooden bowl on the table.

"Think of this," said Mother as she retied the red ribbons that held Poppy's dark curls in bunches beside her round, red cheeks. "If you had a dog, it would only be fair for your brothers and sisters to have pets, too. I can't bear the thought! Seven children and—"

"Seven pets!" Poppy giggled. "Let's."

Mother groaned. "Let's not!"

Poppy let a noodle slide off her spoon and back into her soup. "A dog could sleep in my bunk bed with me, and it wouldn't be underfoot at all. I'd hold it all the time."

Mother sighed. "There are so many of us."
She looked around the tidy, yellow kitchen.
"And this place is so small. How I wish we
could give each of you . . ." She didn't finish
the sentence.

Poppy dreamed aloud. "A curly little dog
would be so cuddly. And it would like me
better than anybody else in the whole world."

Better than anybody else in the whole world, no

9

matter how many brothers and sisters there were, all crowded into the small apartment.

She thought of her best friend, Tink. Tink was an only child. Tink's crayons were always new and long, and she never had to color with little pieces. If Tink got a new dress and wanted tights to match, her mother went straight to Wieboldt's and got them. Tink always got whatever she asked for.

It wasn't fair! Why did some people get everything they wanted while other people always had to think of brothers and sisters and crowded apartments? Poppy made a fist and pushed hard at a scratch on the table. "I wish I was an only child."

"There now," said Mother in her no-nonsense voice. "That's enough, Poppy. We're a big family, and someday you'll know how really nice it is to have sisters and brothers."

She stood up and reached for an envelope on top of the refrigerator. "Get on back to school now, or you'll be late. Drop this in the mailbox on the way."

Poppy spelled out some of the words on the envelope. "P-u-b-l-i-s-h-e-r-s' Ware-house. What's that?"

Mother started clearing away the baking things. "Oh, just something about magazines. Now run along."

Poppy stepped around Little Woody. He smiled up at her and held up his arms. "Me, too?" he asked. "Me, too?"

Funny Little Woody. Those were the only words he would say, and somehow he always said them at exactly the right time. Mostly, he made Poppy laugh. But not right now. Right now, Poppy wanted a curly, cuddly dog and knew she couldn't have one. Right now, Poppy did not feel like laughing.

Mother picked him up. "No, not you, too," she said, lifting him high until he squealed. "Poppy's going back to school. Say bye-bye to Big Sister."

Little Woody just hid his face against Mother and yawned.

The hall door was open. Poppy stepped

around Chryssie and Daisy. They were playing with their trucks, giving rides to Teddy Eddie and Muffer, the stuffed animals that went everywhere with them.

"EEE-eee-EEE," said Chryssie, sounding like a fire truck.

"Pow," said Daisy, banging her truck into the fire truck.

Poppy ran downstairs, thinking about being an only child.

If she were an only child, there would be just Mother and Daddy and her. There would be lots of room for a dog or a cat or a parakeet. There would be room for all three!

A voice echoed down the stairway. "Bye-bye, Poppy."

Poppy looked up from the first-floor hall. Daisy had pushed Muffer through the railing on the third-floor landing and was moving his arm. "Bye-bye," she called again.

Seeing Daisy wave made Poppy feel funny about wanting to be an only child. Then she thought again about having a pet of her very own. A pet who would come just to her, not to anybody else.

"I do wish I was an only child," she thought. "I do. I do. I do." She went outside and closed the door firmly behind her.

2

"Hey, Cat!"

Tink was outside. She lived in a tall, brown brick house just a few doors away.

Big old houses that once had been grand lined both sides of the narrow, curving street. Some had round towers at the corners. A few had pointy iron fences in front. Most had pretty colored glass in the windows.

Long ago each house had held a well-to-do family. Then the rich families moved away and the houses were divided into apartments. Now each house held two or three families, or more.

14

Tink was hopping around on one foot, jumping from one uncracked place in the sidewalk to another. Tink always waited for Poppy after lunch, or Poppy waited for her.

She grinned at Poppy. "You must have drunk your soup through a straw. Come on, pokey."

Poppy ran down the steps. "Well, it isn't easy getting noodles and carrots through a straw," she said seriously. "Especially the carrots."

Tink giggled.

Just seeing Tink made Poppy feel better. Her angry thoughts melted like bits of ice in the sun. She wasn't mad at Tink for getting everything she wanted. Tink couldn't help being an only child.

"Let's trade jackets," said Poppy.

They peeled them off, and the cold spring wind touched Poppy's bare arms. Quickly she slid into Tink's green jacket, thinking how cozy it was to put on a jacket that was already warm from somebody else.

She smoothed the orange and yellow flowers on the front. "I love flowers on jackets."

"Well, I love red," said Tink, zipping up Poppy's red jacket. "My mother says it's death on redheads, though. So I guess I'll never have a red anything." Then she added, "When I grow up, I'm going to change this horrible hair. I'm going to make it honey blond, like the picture on that bottle in Walgreens."

It was a game they played. Poppy took her turn. "When I grow up, I'm going to have a dog and a cat and a horse and some goldfish and a parakeet. I'll let the parakeet fly around my house, and I'll teach it to say 'Scat, cat.'"

"I'm going to wear earrings down to here." Tink touched her shoulders.

"I'm going to have just one child," said Poppy. "And if she wants a—a—rhinoceros, I'll say, 'Well, of course you may have a rhinoceros. Are you sure you wouldn't like two?'"

"I'm going to have boys and girls and maybe even twins," said Tink. Her eyes seemed to be looking into that faraway day. "And I won't ever leave them alone on Saturday night. I'll stay home, and we'll make popcorn and watch TV together."

They came to Halsted Street, and Poppy dropped Mother's letter into the mailbox on the corner. The lid squeaked loudly. It nearly drowned out another squeak nearby, an echoey squeak. She didn't move, listening.

There it was again!

The noise—not a squeak at all, but a very clear *meow*—came from the trash can next to the mailbox.

"There's a cat in there!" she said.

Poppy and Tink stood on tiptoes, pushed the swinging door, and peeked inside. A small, gray, green-eyed cat stared up at them from among the ice-cream wrappers and pop cans.

"Hey, cat," Poppy said gently. "What are you doing in there?" She reached for the little cat, but her arms weren't long enough. She couldn't quite touch it.

"Meow," said the cat and batted at the tips of her fingers.

"We can't leave her," Poppy said. "What'll we do?"

"Wait," said Tink.

She darted down the gangway next to the grocery store on the corner and came back dragging a cardboard box. "Maybe you can stand on this and reach inside."

Poppy stood on the box and reached down into the trash can. She picked up the wriggling little animal. It hissed fiercely, as fiercely as a small cat could.

"I'd hiss, too," Poppy said soothingly. "I'd even bite if someone put me in a trash can.

"She didn't bite me," she said, hopping down from the box. "I think that means she likes me."

"Well, I think it means you're dreaming," said Tink, grinning. She reached out and touched the silky fur.

Poppy cuddled the little cat. She could feel its bones under its fur. "Poor skinny baby," she whispered. "How did you get in there, any-way?"

"Mean kids," said Tink.

Poppy kept on talking to the little cat. "Who feeds you? Who takes care of you? Where's your mother?"

"Dead, I bet," said Tink. "Killed by a car."

With a loud *chink*, the traffic light on the corner changed. Tink looked up. "Hey, it's green. Let's go. We're late."

They ran across busy Halsted Street. And for the rest of the way to Chester P. Armbruster School, Poppy talked to her new friend.

Warm and safe in her arms, the little cat began to purr, a comfortable deep-inside buzzing sound. Poppy could feel the sound. Oh, but it felt nice to hold a purring cat!

"What a pretty face she's got. And just one white paw." Poppy touched the paw. "I wonder if someone's looking for her."

But who could know that?

"The city's full of stray cats," said Tink.

At school, Poppy held the little cat against her cheek. "I wish you could be mine," she whispered.

Tink held the door. "Come on, Popp." A bell rang inside the building.

Poppy set down the little animal. "Goodbye, little cat. Don't let any more mean kids get hold of you." Then she and Tink went inside.

On tiptoes, Poppy looked back through the window in the door. The little cat still sat on the sidewalk. She looked up at Poppy with round baby-cat eyes.

"Poor baby," thought Poppy. "All alone in the city. I wish . . . Oh, I wish . . . "

She didn't finish.

The apartment was too small. There wasn't room. Not for a dog. Not for a cat.

3

Oh, to Be an Only Child

In the days that followed, Poppy saw cats everywhere. But none was gray with just one white paw. None had eyes as green as Lake Michigan after a storm. None was as small as the little gray cat.

"Even her bones felt little," Poppy said, remembering. "As though if you held her too tight she might break. She felt so kind of helpless."

"She sure liked you to hold her," Tink said comfortingly. "Maybe she'll come back . . . "

Then one day the little cat did come back, and Poppy did hold her. It happened after school. The little cat ran up the tree in the schoolyard and stayed there. Some boys threw a stone, and she jumped onto the fire escape.

Poppy's throat felt tight. The fire escape,

made of iron bars, was scary. A little cat could slip between them and fall a long, long way to the ground. Poppy bit her lip, watching, wondering what to do.

After a minute she knew. She ran back into school and found the custodian sweeping the first-grade room.

Mr. Swenson was a cross-looking man. The corners of his mouth turned down even when he wasn't mad about something. Everyone was afraid of him.

Poppy remembered the time she squirted water from the drinking fountain at Joey Busch because he had squirted water at her.

Mr. Swenson had seen her. His bushy black eyebrows knit together. "You don't play with the bubblers in my school," he had said, scowling, handing her the rag he carried. He pointed at the drops of water around the fountain. "Make dry!"

Poppy had wiped away the water. And she had stayed out of Mr. Swenson's way ever since.

But today she needed his help.

"Please, Mr. Swenson." Her voice, thin and shaky, echoed in the empty room. "Will you get a little cat that's stuck on the fire escape?"

"Huh?" Mr. Swenson grunted. Then, grumbling to himself, he followed her to the door and looked outside. Without a word, he turned and went upstairs to the fifth-grade room.

Poppy trotted after him.

He opened the window and scooped up the little cat from the fire escape.

The cat hissed, and Mr. Swenson said something that sounded like a bad word. He gave the cat to Poppy and rubbed a scratch on his hand.

"You teach that cat of yours she shouldn't climb on my school," he said.

"But she isn't my—"

Mr. Swenson didn't let her finish. "You mind now. No back talk."

"Yes, Mr. Swenson," whispered Poppy.

She petted the little cat. "I saved you twice,"

she said. "I guess that means something. I guess you *are* my cat."

But—what would Mother say?

"Well, ask her," said Tink as they walked home. "Maybe she'll change her mind. Mine does all the time. Just last week she said she'd smack me if I came in after six o'clock. Well, I did, and she didn't."

It was true. Mothers did change their minds. That very morning Mother had said Poppy must wear her warm winter jacket. Then she had listened to the weatherman and said Poppy could wear her spring jacket, after all.

"Tell her . . . tell her a cat will catch the mice in your house." Tink was trying to be helpful.

"No!" said Poppy. "She won't hurt mice!"

"Bet she will," said Tink. "She's a cat and that's what cats do."

Poppy thought of something. "You helped find her. I guess she's sort of your cat, too. I'll bet you could keep her at your house—if you wanted to."

"But she likes *you*," said Tink, "so she's your cat. And anyway, I've got eleven stuffed animals."

Eleven stuffed animals weren't the same at all. But Poppy didn't tell Tink that. She was glad Tink didn't want the little gray cat.

The boys were in the downstairs hall at Poppy's house—Fielding, the oldest; Wilding, exactly one year, four months, and eight days older than Poppy; and Forrest, just a little kid, still in first grade.

Forrest was on the floor, turning the pages of *Super Micro-Boy*. He looked up. "Hey, Popp. Whatcha got?"

Wilding was looking at one of Forrest's comic books, too, but with a magnifying glass. He held the glass up to one eye, which became huge. "I, Wilding the Mag-ni-fi-cent, could use a cat in my magic act."

Fielding was unlocking his bike from the radiator. It was time to deliver his newspapers. "Forget it," he said. "Ma won't let you keep a cat."

Fielding was always saying "You can't . . . you better not . . . it won't work."

Poppy hugged the little cat. "Maybe Mom will change her mind."

"Good . . . luck," said Fielding. The words sounded like stones dropping into a dark pond.

"Come upstairs with me," Poppy whispered to Tink. Sometimes mothers didn't say no when other people were around.

Mother was sewing at the dining-room table. "Change into play shoes, Poppy," she said, not looking up.

Daisy and Chryssie's eyes grew round.

"A little bitty kitty," said Daisy, taking her thumb out of her mouth.

Chryssie took her thumb out of her mouth, too.

"Did you bring the kitty for us?" she asked, popping her thumb back into her mouth as soon as she stopped talking.

"Me, too. Me, too," came a piping voice near Poppy's feet. Little Woody peeked out from under the table.

Mother looked up. She rested her head on the sewing machine. "Mercy me, Poppy! If I've told you once, I've told you a dozen times—no animals in the house."

"She'd be awful nice for the little kids when I'm at school," Poppy said hopefully.

Mother shook her head. "*No, Poppy.*"

"She wouldn't be one single bit of trouble."

"No. No. No," said Mother in her I-mean-it voice. "Now you just take the cat back where you found it."

Poppy looked at Tink. How could you take a cat back to a trash can? Or to a fire escape?

As Poppy and Tink left the dining room, Mother was saying, "Big girls don't suck their thumbs. Daisy, here's some paper. Why don't you draw a picture? Chryssie, can you make a picture, too? We'll tape them on the refrigerator for everyone to see."

On the landing, Tink said, "Wow! Your mother sure doesn't change her mind."

They went downstairs, and Poppy sat on the bottom step.

Fielding put on his rain poncho and hung his bike chains over his shoulder. "Told you so," he said, opening the street door. Thunder growled. The door bumped shut behind him.

Poppy dug a bubblegum wrapper out of her pocket. She rolled it into a ball and tossed it onto the floor. The little cat jumped on it.

No one spoke.

"She feels as if she's mine," Poppy said after a while. "She likes me and I like her."

The little cat batted the paper ball. Poppy and Tink watched her.

A voice called down from the top of the house. "Mamma says everyone should come up and change into play shoes."

Forrest went upstairs, still looking at his comic book.

Wilding put down the magnifying glass and held out a grubby deck of cards. "Here, Popp. Take a card, any card."

Poppy didn't feel like doing magic tricks. But old Wilding was trying to make her feel better. She took a card.

Wilding closed his eyes and held his hands to his head. "I, Wilding the Stu-pen-dous, am thinking of a card. It is . . . it is . . . Is it the six of hearts?" He opened his eyes, looking hopeful.

Poppy shook her head. "Uh-uh. Eight of clubs."

"Aw, rats," he said. "Well, I'll get it right next time."

He stuffed the cards into his pocket and went up the stairs two at a time.

"I better go," Tink said softly. "My mother really yells if I'm not there when she gets home from work."

The wet, plopping sound of rain filled the hall for a minute as she went out.

Poppy held the little cat against her cheek. "Want to stay here in the hall for a while?" she whispered. "I'll come back as soon as I change shoes." And she went upstairs.

She looked down from the landing. The little cat was exploring under the radiator in the empty hall. How small she looked!

Just then the first-floor apartment door opened. Mrs. Guschelbauer came out with trash. She saw the little cat.

"Ach," she said, "animals in the house make the landlord mad." She picked up the cat by the back of the neck, opened the door, and dropped her outside.

As soon as Mrs. Guschelbauer went back into her apartment, Poppy flew down the stairs, swinging around the newel posts at the landings. Poor little cat! Thrown out into the rain as though nobody cared.

"I care," thought Poppy, pulling open the front door. "I care."

Rain pounded the steps. Thunder cracked loudly and she jumped. She stared into the wet grayness, up the street, down the street. The little cat was nowhere to be seen.

Poppy leaned against the door, watching the splashing, spattering rain. She didn't even notice that she was getting wet.

Oh, to be an only child . . . an only child . . . an only child . . .

4

Alone with Daddy

Poppy's eyes opened. The light in the bedroom was dim. It was very early in the morning.

She crawled to the end of her bunk bed and pulled aside the window shade. Where was the little gray cat?

There were puddles on the sidewalk, but the rain had stopped and the sky was a pale pinky blue. It was going to be a nice day. She looked up and down the street.

No little cat stalked along the sidewalk, its tail pointing at the sky.

No little cat sat on a porch anywhere, licking one white paw.

Where had she gone?

Quietly Poppy slid down from the top bunk and gathered up her clothes.

Daisy and Chryssie, their thumbs in their mouths, were asleep in the bottom bunk.

Wilding and Forrest were asleep in their bunks on the boys' side of the bedroom.

Nobody heard her tiptoe out of the bedroom.

Fielding was asleep on the rollaway bed in the living room. He was snoring softly.

Mother didn't hear her tiptoe past the bedroom door.

And Little Woody, asleep in his crib in the dining room, didn't hear her, either.

Everyone was asleep except Poppy.

Softly she closed the kitchen door and got dressed.

She found her jacket in the back hall and went down the back stairs. Just as she touched the doorknob, the door opened. Daddy came in from work.

"Whoa-there," he said. "Where are you going at this hour, Sis?" He put his hand on top of her head and turned her around. "Come upstairs and talk to your old dad."

Poppy went with him. His hand rested so firmly on her head she couldn't do anything else.

She felt all mixed up. She wanted to go outside and hunt for the little gray cat. But she wanted to talk to Daddy, too. She hardly ever had him all to herself, and it made her feel warm and happy to be all alone with him.

They went upstairs into the kitchen. Daddy turned on the light and sat down at the table. He took off his shoes, sighing, and dropped them on the floor.

Poppy opened his lunch bucket. The red plastic jars for soup and potato salad were empty. So was the Thermos. But there was half a meat-loaf sandwich and an orange, one of the big sweet kind Mother bought just for Daddy's lunches.

More than anything, Poppy liked sandwiches left over from Daddy's lunches. And this morning she didn't even have to be unselfish and share, because nobody else was around to say, "I want some, too."

Daddy began to peel the orange. "Okay. In twenty-five words or less, tell me about getting up early."

Poppy told him all about the little gray cat. "Mom says I can't keep her. Only I've *got* her. I mean, I saved her two times. And . . ."

Daddy pulled the orange apart and laid the pieces on the table between them. He put a piece in his mouth and took a stack of contest blanks from under the apple bowl.

"Well now, Sis, Mom's right. There're too many of us around here to have animals running in and out. I guess you've got to forget about having an indoors cat."

It was the way he said "indoors cat" that lit an idea in Poppy's mind. Her brown eyes sparkled. "You mean, I can't have an indoors cat, but I can have an *outdoors* one?"

The little cat would belong to her, just her. It would love her more than anyone else. It would be her very own particular pet friend. Poppy sighed happily at the thought. "She could be all mine for real."

Daddy wrote something on one of the contest blanks. "Don't be too sure about that 'real' business," he said. "Cats come and go. But she might hang around the yard if you treat her nice."

Stretching and yawning, he waved the contest paper. "Maybe I'll win one of these big ones someday. We'll be rich, and we'll rent a bigger place. Then you can have a cat that's an indoors-outdoors cat."

Poppy felt hopeful and happy. "Maybe it'll happen," she said, leaning on the table. "You won the Hostess-Saver Server Set and the case of pop. Maybe you'll win again. Maybe you'll win a big one."

Waking-up sounds came from the front of the house.

Bare feet pattered on the floor.

"All right, you wise guys. Who hid my shoes?" That was Fielding.

A giggle. That was Wilding.

A wail. "I want Muffer. Muffer got lost in the night." That was Daisy.

"Look under the covers." That was Mother. "Fielding, you've outgrown those jeans. Put on the ones I mended yesterday."

"Aw, Ma, they aren't too . . ."

"No arguments."

Mother came into the kitchen. She kissed Daddy. "Morning, Gar."

Daddy hugged her and patted her back.

The nice time alone with Daddy was ended. Sunshine coming in the window splashed the kitchen floor with brightness.

Poppy leaned against Daddy. "Now can I go out?" she whispered.

Daddy looked at his watch. "Okay," he said.

So Poppy went outside to find her very own outdoors cat.

5

The Best Outdoors Cat

The sun was shining, but it was nippy cold, anyway. Poppy shivered and zipped up her red jacket as she looked up and down the street. No cat was to be seen—not in front of the house or in the side yard or in the backyard.

"Kitty-kitty-kitty," she called.

No little cat came running to be picked up.

She went down to the corner. No little cat was in the trash can. She was glad of that.

An old lady got off the Number 8 Halsted bus and came plodding up Greenbrier Street. She carried two shopping bags. Rags spilled out of them. She walked as though her feet hurt.

A little boy came out of a house across the street. He had a whole box of Froot Loops. He sat on the top step and stuffed them into his mouth, handful after handful.

The door behind Poppy opened. Fielding came out, on his way to deliver his papers. He bumped his bike down the steps.

A man came out of the house next door. He unlocked a van, got in, and started the engine. With the first sound, a small gray animal shot out from under the front end.

"Cat!" yelled Poppy. She darted into the street and picked up the little cat.

The man in the van blew his horn and yelled, "Don't *do* that, kid. Wanta get killed?"

"Hey," said Fielding, "that's a pretty smart cat. A car's warm for a while after it stops. So she stayed under there, maybe on top of one of the tires."

"She's an extra-specially smart cat," Poppy said proudly.

Fielding laughed. "Of course, she's kind of dumb, too."

Poppy stared at him.

He swung onto his bike. "I mean," he said over his shoulder, "if she doesn't get out fast enough when the car starts—zap! No more cat."

Poppy watched him ride away. Why did Fielding always think of such awful things?

She opened her jacket and tucked the little cat inside, against her sweatshirt.

Wilding came outside, swinging his swimming bag. "Found her, huh? Watcha gonna do with her?"

"She's going to be my outdoors cat," Poppy said. She remembered the wet, cold night. "I'm going to find her a dry place to sleep. And I'm going to teach her to be the best outdoors cat that ever was."

"How you gonna feed her?" asked Wilding.

Poppy didn't have an answer. How *would* she feed a cat? There were just too many things to think about all at once!

"Wait a sec," said Wilding. He ran into the house. When he came back he carried a milk carton and a small aluminum-foil dish. "Ma didn't see me take this," he said. Then he hurried away, whistling, to Saturday morning Porpoise Class.

Wi was the best old brother!

Poppy poured the milk into the shiny foil dish and set it on the sidewalk. She put the little cat down beside her breakfast.

Tink came outside just then. She looked surprised. "Your cat's still here."

"She'll come back again, too," Poppy said happily. "Animals always come back when you feed them."

Together they watched the little cat drink the milk, her pink tongue moving so fast it could hardly be seen. And Poppy told Tink about having an outdoors cat, the best one that ever was.

"You'd better name her," said Tink. "You can't just call her *cat*. Every cat will come when you call—millions and trillions of them."

Poppy could almost see jillions of cats pouring into Greenbrier Street. She laughed.

Tink was thinking. "Fluffy? You could call her Fluffy."

Poppy shook her head. "She isn't fluffy." Her forehead wrinkled as she thought. "I guess she should have a flower name, like everyone in our family." She tried a few names, slowly. "Violet . . . Lily . . . Daffodil . . ."

"You could call her Daffy for short," suggested Tink.

They giggled. But they decided against Daffodil.

Tulip . . . Sweet Pea . . . Dandelion—none was just right.

The little cat finished her milk. She set a paw in the dish and licked around the edges.

A door slammed and awful Jane Ellen ran across the street to see what was going on. Horrible, terrible Jane Ellen. Sometimes she called Poppy "Petunia" and Tink "Tin Can." If she had Cracker Jack she looked right at people while she ate it and never offered to share. She always pushed to be first in line, and she cheated at hopscotch, too.

Jane Ellen watched the little cat lick her paw and rub it over her face and ears.

"My mother says cats carry germs," sniffed Jane Ellen.

"They don't!" Poppy was outraged. "Cats are extra-special spick-and-span clean. Everyone knows that."

Jane Ellen swung back and forth on the stair railing, watching. "Who'd want an old cat? I can't stand cats. And you can't keep her, any- way. Landlords never let you have pets."

"I am going to keep her," said Poppy. "But not indoors. She's my outdoors cat."

Jane Ellen stopped swinging and stared at Poppy. "That's dumb. Whoever heard of an outdoors cat! She'll run away."

"She won't," said Poppy. "I'm going to find her a place to sleep and help her find food to eat. I'm going to teach her to watch out for cars."

"You can't teach a cat those things," said Jane Ellen. "She'll run away. A car will hit her and she'll get squashed." She said "squashed" as though she liked the word.

Poppy picked up the little cat.

Tink gathered up the dish and the milk carton.

"Get lost, Jane Ellen," said Poppy.

"Go play in the traffic, Jane Ellen," said
Tink.

Poppy and Tink went to find a sleeping
place for the little cat.

"Can't keep an outdoors cat!" Jane Ellen's
voice followed them. "Can't! Can't! Can't!"

I can, thought Poppy. *I will. I will. I will.*

6

The Little-Steps House

There weren't many good places for a cat to sleep.

"Under the front steps?" asked Tink.

"Too many people walk past," said Poppy. "Especially old Jane Ellen." She made a face.

There were deep places next to the basement windows. "But she'd get wet when it rained," said Poppy.

"And big dogs might jump on her," said Tink.

Poppy led the way to the backyard, looking around.

"Under the back steps?" asked Tink.

"The sides are closed," said Poppy. She

looked more closely. What was that dark line back near the wall?

She pushed aside the lilac branches and touched the dark line. "It's a crack," she called.

She tugged at the cracked board. It wiggled. She pushed and pulled. The board creaked and came away in two pieces. She tugged at another board and after a while it broke away, too.

Tink wiggled into the narrow place beside Poppy. "What's in there?"

The dark space under the steps was striped with ribbons of sunlight. Poppy reached in and touched the ground. "It's dry," she said. "There's just one stiff old weed from last summer. It's a pretty good sleeping place for a cat."

The little cat was following a bug with her nose. Poppy picked her up and the bug was safe.

"Here,"she said, putting the cat inside, "this is your little-steps house."

The little cat nosed into the dark corners. She batted at the weed with a paw. Then she came back out into the sunshine.

"Hey, cat," said Tink. "That's where you're supposed to sleep."

Poppy put the little cat into her house again—and she came right back outside. She stood up on her back legs and pulled her claws down the trunk of the lilac bush.

Poppy rested on her heels. "I guess it doesn't look like a house in there." She thought. "If I was a cat, I'd want something soft to sleep on in my house."

"An old jacket, maybe?" asked Tink. "Have you got one?"

Poppy shook her head. "My mom packs things away for the twins to grow into. Have you got one?"

Tink didn't. "My mom sends all my old stuff to my Aunt Pam for Jenny."

"I've got some money," Poppy said thoughtfully. "My Grandpa gave me some. And I saved some when we sold those aluminum cans."

"Lots?" asked Tink. "Enough to buy something?"

"Wait," said Poppy.

She ran indoors. When she came back she had two quarters, three dimes, three nickels, and six pennies in her hand. She gathered up the little cat.

"Where are we going?" asked Tink. "What can we get for a dollar and one cent?"

"Maybe something," said Poppy. "You'll see."

Up Greenbrier Street, around the curve, onto Clark Street—Poppy led the way. She stopped in front of the Red Shield Resale Store and looked in the window. Lots of Saturday shoppers were inside.

She felt shy and scared. She had never come shopping all by herself. Maybe the people would ask why she wanted a jacket. Maybe they wouldn't sell something just for a cat.

A tug on her sweatshirt made her look down. The little cat's claws were stuck. She looked up at Poppy with round, unblinking eyes. "Meow," she said.

She looked so soft and helpless. Poppy felt

full of love. She knew she could go into the store all by herself.

"Here," she said to Tink, unhooking the stuck claws.

Now Tink knew what Poppy was going to do. She cuddled the little cat. "Get something pretty," she whispered. "We'll wait out here."

Inside the store, Poppy went to the place where the clothes were. She tried to look as though she shopped like this every day.

She pushed past dresses on racks. Sweaters were piled on a table. A sweater would be warm and snuggly. A sweater would be exactly right.

She held up a blue one, the way Mother did when she shopped.

"Oh, that's too big for you, honey," said a voice. "Girls' clothes are over there, near the baby things."

Poppy wanted to disappear in a puff of smoke, like a magic genie. But she had to stay. She looked up at the woman. "Well," she whispered, "it—uh—isn't for me."

The woman smiled. "Oh," she said. "A

present for someone. That's nice! For a lady or a man?"

Did it matter that the present was for a lady *cat*? "A lady," said Poppy, crossing her fingers in case that was a lie.

The woman held up a gray sweater with pink flowers on the front. "This has hardly been worn. Does it look as if it might fit?"

"It looks big enough," said Poppy quite truthfully.

"Does she wear gray?" asked the woman.

Poppy uncrossed her fingers. "Oh, yes!"

The woman read the tag on the sweater. "A dollar forty-nine."

"Oh-h-h." Poppy's voice drooped. The sweater cost too much. She reached for a brown one.

"How much do you have, honey?" the woman asked kindly.

Poppy opened her hand. The woman looked at the money. "Well," she said thoughtfully, "since this is a present, I guess it can go for a dollar and one cent."

She pulled off the tag and gave the sweater to Poppy.

Poppy hugged it. The gray wool felt soft and warm and bunchy. "Oh, thank you," she whispered, and she ran out of the store before the woman could change her mind.

"Got it," she said proudly, holding up the sweater for Tink to see.

"There's pink on it," sighed Tink. "Oh, I do love pink."

They hurried home and started to put the sweater under the steps. Then Tink had an idea. "It'll get dirty! Wait!"

She ran out of the yard. A few minutes later she came back carrying a box. "From the corner store," she said, panting.

Poppy laughed. "Look!" She pointed at the words on the box: *Rosebud • Heart of the Harvest • Fancy Celery Hearts*. "Rosebud's a flower name!"

She held the little cat against her cheek. "Rosebud-Cat, that's your name. And there's your bed."

Tink pulled another board away from the steps and pushed the box into the opening. She put the sweater in the box. And then Poppy put Rosebud into the cozy box-bed.

Rosebud walked in a circle and patted the sweater. Then she curled up on it and closed her eyes.

The little cat had a name. She had a little-steps house. She had a bed with her very own name on it.

And Poppy had an outdoors cat.

7
What Rosebud Needed to Know

Mornings before school Poppy filled Rosebud's water dish. Some days she left a piece of lunch meat or some milk under the steps. More often she left an empty tunafish or soup can. "It's empty," she would say, "but you can lick it anyway, Rosie-bud."

The little cat licked greedily at the cans.

After school Poppy and Tink played with Rosebud.

The little cat liked paper and string. She followed a string dragged in front of her. Eyes narrow, she walked on silent paws, watching it. Suddenly she would jump and catch the string.

When Poppy tossed a ball of paper, Rosebud caught it. She lay on her back and rolled it in her four paws. Sometimes she even brought it back to Poppy and dropped it at her feet.

"That's because she likes you," said Tink.

Poppy felt sunshiny inside. For it was true. Rosebud liked her more than anybody.

The days grew warm. The grass turned green. Bugs came out of cracks in the sidewalks and moved in the sun.

Rosebud followed the bugs, her nose so close she was nearly cross-eyed. Sometimes she put a paw on a bug and then looked surprised when she lifted the paw and the bug was still.

Poppy tried to tell her about bugs. "You musn't hurt bugs, Rosebud. Do—not—hurt —little—bugs."

But Rosebud only put out her pink tongue and washed her face.

Birds flew about looking for food and bits of string to make nests.

Rosebud stared at them, her eyes thin slits. Once Poppy saw her walk slowly and silently toward a robin.

"Fly, bird!" she yelled. "No, Rosebud!"

The robin flew into a tree and Rosebud sat very still, looking up at it.

Poppy picked her up. She talked right into Rosebud's face. "It's a bad thing to scare birds. *No*, Rosebud. *No!*"

Rosebud put out her tongue and touched Poppy's chin. She seemed to be listening. But she looked at birds, anyway.

There were lots and lots of things to teach a cat who lived outdoors in the city.

"She needs to know how to cross the street," said Tink. "She's gonna get killed if she's not careful."

So they tried to teach Rosebud to cross the street at the corner. They practiced on Halsted Street, until old Mr. Frickensmith came out of his store. He glared at them.

"You, kids," he yelled. "You want to be flat kids, eh? You want a flat cat, too, I suppose. You want to get killed, eh? That's gonna happen if you play in the street. Now go somewhere else. I can't stand it."

Poppy and Tink went down to Broadway. Again they tried to get Rosebud to follow them across the street at the corner.

But Rosebud wouldn't. She ran under a parked car. Then when the light turned red—exactly at the most dangerous time—she dashed across the street, zigzagging among the moving cars.

Tink watched her. "She sure is fast."

"Maybe she's so fast," said Poppy, "she doesn't need to learn to cross at the corner."

They had to give up. They couldn't teach Rosebud about corners and stoplights. But there were other things she needed to learn.

"I wonder what she eats besides what you feed her," Tink said one day as they sat on the steps in front of her house. "Birds, do you suppose?"

"No!" said Poppy. "I just know she wouldn't eat a bird."

"Well, I just know cats do eat birds," Tink said matter-of-factly. "And anyway, birds are pretty dumb if they let cats catch 'em. I mean, birds can get away. They can fly."

Perhaps what Tink said was true. Poppy knew she couldn't give Rosebud enough food.

What if her outdoors cat really was eating birds! That was too awful to think about.

She held up Rosebud and looked right into her green eyes. "I wish I could feed you more," she said sadly.

Where was there food, free food?

"Leftovers?" asked Tink.

"Not at our house," said Poppy. She laughed. "Nothing's ever left over. My mother always shops at Columbo's sales, and she still says she can hardly make ends meet."

"Columbo's!" Tink sat up straight. "Have you ever been around at the back?"

Poppy shook her head.

"Well, they put boxes and stuff outside," said Tink. "Maybe they toss out good food."

Free food, maybe, for Rosebud?

Tink and Poppy hurried down Greenbrier Street and turned onto Broadway. Watching for cars, they cut through Columbo's parking lot and went to the back of the store.

The stockroom boys were dragging boxes outside. Poppy and Tink waited until they finished, then went close to a pile of cartons and bags set near one of the Dumpster carts.

Poppy's nose wrinkled. "Ugh! Un-perfume," she said as she set Rosebud down.

They watched the little cat.

She sniffed at an empty meat can and poked at a box that said "Fresh Shrimp from the Gulf."

She jumped on some paper and rattled it noisily.

Then she turned over a box, and there was a nice fresh fish head. She began to eat hungrily.

"It's got eyes," said Tink. "I can't look."

"Rosebud thinks it's pretty good," said Poppy.

Rosebud finished the fish head. Daintily she licked her paws clean.

Poppy picked her up. "If we bring Rosebud back here," she said, "and she learns to come by herself, she'll always have someplace to find food."

And then Rosebud would never, never have to eat a bug or a mouse or a bird. Not ever.

8

The Good Things about Rosebud

One Saturday afternoon, Poppy sat on the front steps playing tic-tac-toe with a stubby piece of chalk. She had just found out you can't play tic-tac-toe by yourself. You always come out even.

Rosebud was playing with a tin can on the sidewalk. The can made a cheerful clanking noise.

Mother came outside. She was wearing lipstick and carried her purse. "Oh, there you are," she said. "Come along, baby. I'm running up to the resale store. It's a good time for winter bargains."

Usually Poppy liked shopping with Mother. But not today. Not at the resale store. What if the sweater woman was there? What if she remembered Poppy and asked if "the lady" liked her present? What would Poppy say? Would she have to say the sweater was for a lady *cat?* Would the sweater woman be angry? And what would Mother say if she found out how Poppy had spent her savings?

She drew a circle with her chalk. Perfectly round circles were lucky. But this circle had one crooked side.

"Poppy, what's got into you?" asked Mother. "You know you like to go shopping. Now come along. Let's see if we can find you a coat for next winter."

Poppy followed Mother up the street, dragging her feet and looking back at Rosebud. The little cat was still playing with the tin can.

A car was out in front of the resale store, and two men were carrying in a TV set. Clothes and a lamp were inside the car.

"There'll be a lot of new things today," said

Mother. "People clear out their closets when winter's over."

They went inside. Mother looked at a coffee table and a mirror and a four-slice toaster. "Daddy could put a new cord on the toaster, I think," she said. But she didn't buy it.

Poppy looked around, staying close beside Mother. Lots of people were in the store. Then she saw the sweater woman.

Poppy ducked her head. Maybe the woman wouldn't see her.

Mother led the way to a corner where girls' clothes hung on racks. She held up a coat. "Almost like new," she said. "Let's see if it fits."

Poppy put on the coat. It was red with an edge of navy blue around the collar and down the front. She patted the red buttons. She felt dressed up.

Mother turned up the sleeves. "It's a little big. But you'll grow some before next winter."

Someone was coming toward them. Poppy looked at the floor, at the jars under a table, and at the feet that stopped beside Mother.

"Need help here?" asked the owner of the feet.

Poppy peeked. The sweater woman!

"We'll just try a few more of these coats," said Mother. "Here, baby, try this brown one."

Still looking at the floor, Poppy poked her arms into a brown coat. The sleeves didn't cover her wrists, and her shoulders felt scrunched together.

"Well, that doesn't fit," said Mother and helped her into a blue-and-white checked coat.

It was very hard to try on coats and keep her head down. Besides, Poppy felt like a baby, being stuffed into coats and buttoned up.

"You'd outgrow this one by next winter," said Mother. "Let's try the red one again. And hold up your head. Mercy me, what has gotten into you today, Poppy!"

The woman leaned down to help button the coat. She looked into Poppy's face. "Why, hello there! Did—"

Poppy held her breath. She looked scared.

The woman stopped in the middle of her

question. She looked from Poppy to Mother, and then she winked at Poppy. "Do you like the red one?"

Poppy breathed a big sigh. "Oh yes," she said.

And that's how she got her next winter's coat.

"A wonderful bargain," said Mother, on the way home. "Why, it's almost like new!"

When they got near the house, Poppy saw Rosebud. She was coming around the corner of the house carrying something in her mouth. She came to Poppy and laid it at her feet.

"A bird!" cried Poppy. "Rosebud, you mustn't hurt birds!"

Poppy picked up the bird and sat on the steps, holding it. Rosebud wrapped herself around Poppy's ankles, purring. Then she sat and washed her paws.

The bird didn't look hurt. It felt soft and ruffly, but it didn't move. It was dead.

"It's a sparrow," said Poppy. Tears slid down her cheeks. "Rosebud caught it and—"

Mother sat on the step and hugged Poppy. "Part of being a cat is catching things," she said.

"Not birds," Poppy said firmly.

"Yes, birds," said Mother. "And mice and bugs. Rosebud isn't mean. She just does what's natural for a cat."

"I don't like her to catch birds," said Poppy.

Mother was quiet. She patted Poppy's hair. "Baby, you can't change that part of Rosebud. But you like other things about her, don't you?"

Poppy nodded.

"Tell me," said Mother.

Poppy swallowed. "She's soft. And she purrs. And she plays and makes me laugh. And she likes me."

"Those are all good things," said Mother. "But you have to take the bad with the good and like her all the same."

"I *love* Rosebud," Poppy said softly.

"She brought the bird to you because she was proud of catching it," said Mother. "She must love you, too." She hugged Poppy again. "Try not to feel too bad," she said. Then she went indoors to pick up the twins and Little Woody from Mrs. Guschelbauer.

Poppy still held the sparrow. "I'm sorry, sputzie," she whispered. "I'll bury you in my gold candy box." She dried her eyes with the back of her hand.

Rosebud was playing with Poppy's shoelaces. She caught one and tugged on it until the bow came untied.

Poppy patted her. Mother had said Rosebud was proud and wanted to be praised. "Nice cat, Rosie-bud," said Poppy.

Then she looked down at the little brown bird.

"Just the same," she went on, "even if you were acting the way a cat's supposed to—you shouldn't hurt birds."

9

The Most Important Day

It was going to be just about the most important day of all their lives. But nothing about the morning would have led Poppy to guess that.

Mother overslept, and that meant they all slept late and had to hurry. Hurry in the bathroom. Hurry getting dressed. Hurry eating breakfast.

"Where's my jacket?" yelled Fielding.

"I can't find my library book and it's due today," yelled Wilding.

"I need twenty-five cents for paper," yelled Forrest.

"There's a button off my shirt," wailed Poppy.

Daisy and Chryssie and Little Woody trailed into the kitchen.

"Can't find Teddy Eddie," wept Chryssie.

"Want some cereal," said Daisy.

"Me,too," said Little Woody. "Me, too."

Mother clapped her hands over her ears.

Just then the back door opened, and Daddy came in from work. He looked around the crowded kitchen. "Having a party?"

"Oh, Gar," said Mother. "I'm so glad you're home. Take the little ones into the living room, will you? Just till I get the big ones off to school."

"Come on, gang," said Daddy. "We know when we're not wanted." He picked up Little Woody and Chryssie like sacks of potatoes, one under each arm. "I'll read you a story."

Daisy trailed after them, her thumb in her mouth.

"Big girls don't suck their thumbs, Daisy," called Mother.

"Fielding, see if your jacket's in the hall.

"Wilding, I think I saw Little Woody take your book behind the sofa last night.

"Forrest, see if you have enough paper to last until tomorrow. I'm short of change.

"Then everybody sit down and finish your cereal."

Fielding found his jacket. It was behind the dining-room door.

Wilding found his library book. "Woody scribbled in it," he moaned. "What'll I tell the librarian?"

"Tell her you'll erase it," said Mother. "And tell her after this you won't leave books where your baby brother can get them."

Forrest counted the sheets of paper in his notebook. "Maybe if I scrunch up my writing there'll be enough for today," he decided.

Poppy looked at the new button on her shirt. "It doesn't match. It's bigger than the others."

"It will have to do for today," said Mother. "I'll sew another one on tonight. Now all of you, scoot."

They scooted.

Wilding and Fielding could run faster than Poppy. Soon they were halfway down the block.

Poppy could run almost as fast as they

could, but Forrest couldn't keep up. She slowed down to wait for him.

"It feels funny to go into school when everyone's there already," he panted.

"I'll go to your room with you," said Poppy. "Tell Mrs. Ching we all overslept. I don't think she'll scold."

The hall was empty, and their footsteps sounded loud and echoey. They could hear the children in the first-grade room saying the Pledge of Allegiance to the flag.

Poppy waited while Forrest went inside. She peeked through the glass in the door. Mrs. Ching smiled at him, so Poppy knew Forrest wasn't in trouble. She hurried to her own room.

Mrs. Robbin was writing on the board. "You're late this morning, Poppy," she said.

Everybody looked up. Poppy remembered the button that didn't match and moved her arm so nobody could see it. "We didn't wake up in time," she said.

"I see," said Mrs. Robbin. "Well, hurry now and take out your math book."

After that it was a perfectly everyday kind of school day.

In spelling they learned *delicious* and *forest* and *squirrel* and *acorn*. Poppy liked *squirrel* best.

In social studies they talked about George Washington. His horse's name was Nelson.

After recess they did a science experiment with balloons and a yardstick and learned that air has weight. That made chubby TJ laugh.

"Air is fat," he giggled. He blew a paper off his desk. "Fat air."

Everyone began to laugh and blow papers around. "Fat air!" "Fat air!" "Fat air!"

The lunch bell rang.

"Air isn't exactly fat," said Mrs. Robbin. "But it does have weight. We'll talk about it more tomorrow."

Some of the kids went to the cafeteria for lunch, and Poppy went home. She always went home for lunch.

As soon as she opened the street door, she knew something was happening.

Mrs. Guschelbauer was leaning on the stair

railing, looking upward. "Ach, Poppy, you better get upstairs."

Mrs. Jacobs was out on the second floor landing, too, looking up. "Think of that!" She was shaking her head. "Just think of that!"

Wilding leaned over the railing. "Hey, Popp," he yelled. "Hurry up. They're gonna take our picture!"

Poppy ran upstairs and into the apartment. It was crowded with people, all talking.

A pretty lady was talking to Mother and writing in a notebook.

A jolly-looking man with a beard was walking around with a camera. "Come on, kids," he was saying, "try to stop jiggling."

A tall man in a dark suit and a white shirt seemed to fill up the middle of the living room. "Okay, everyone," he kept saying. "Let's get organized here. Everybody? Everybody—all right now, suppose we all gather around Mother there on the sofa. Mother, you look just fine."

Mother's cheeks were pink. She kept patting

her hair. She looked the way she did when they all surprised her on Mother's Day by taking her breakfast in bed.

Poppy tugged at Daddy's hand. "Daddy? What is it? What's happened?"

Daddy looked down at her and blinked, almost as if he didn't see her. "We've won a house," he said. "A brand-new house."

Poppy's mouth fell open. "You mean you won a big contest? Real big, like you said you would someday?"

Daddy shook his head. "I didn't win. *Mother* did. She won a prize from a magazine subscription place."

"A house? A whole house? Of our very own?" Poppy asked.

"Our very own," said Daddy.

And Mother had done it!

10

Their Dumb Old Names

Everybody crowded around the sofa.

The lady with the notebook looked at the group. "Seven children!" she said. "Their names are . . . ?"

"Fielding's the oldest." Mother smiled at each of them in turn. "Then there's Wilding, Poppy, Forrest, the twins Chrysanthemum and Daisy, and Little Woody."

The lady's lips twitched. "But . . . they're all named . . . they sound like . . . I mean, Fielding Flower? And Wilding Flower? And *Forrest* Flower?"

The boys turned red. Poppy squirmed. They didn't like to be teased about their dumb old names.

Mother put her hand on Poppy's arm. "It's what's always been done in my husband's family," she said.

The lady turned to Daddy. "Your name, Mr. Flower?"

Poppy held her breath. Would Daddy tell?

Daddy just grinned. "G.," he said. "G. O."

That's all he would say. And even if the lady looked in the phone book, all she would find was *Flower, G. O.*

The lady glanced around the living room. "Such an attractive room. Those lemon yellow curtains bring the sun right indoors."

Mother smiled.

The lady went on. "Winning a house is a great piece of luck for you. You can certainly use a bigger place."

Mother got the same look Poppy had seen one day when a man at the resale store asked if they needed help. "We get along fine," she said softly, firmly. "Just fine."

Daddy looked proudly at Mother. "My wife's a good manager. We have everything we need and more."

The lady stopped asking questions.

Forrest was hopping up and down in front of

the jolly man with a camera. "Take my picture, mister. Take my picture."

The man did. Then, "All right," he said, "now everyone move in close to your mom."

Little Woody peeked out from behind the sofa. "Me, too!"

Mother picked him up and held him on her lap. They all stared at the camera.

The man looked back at them over the camera. "Never saw such a solemn bunch! You'd think there wasn't going to be any more Christmas. Hey, there—give me a smile."

Poppy tried, but her face was stiff. She felt as if a giant with one great big eye was staring at her and she was supposed to *smile*.

"What we need is a joke," said the tall man. "Say something funny, Art."

"Bellybutton," said Art.

Everybody giggled, and he took their picture. "That's more like it," he said.

Then he took pictures of Mother by herself—watering her plants, sewing a dress for Poppy, reading a magazine.

The tall man gave Mother a paper he called a floor plan. "Got just the land for that new house of yours, too," he said. "Out west of Downers Grove. The country will be great for the kids."

Then he and the lady and the man with the beard put away their notebooks and cameras and went away.

Daddy closed the door. "Ya-hooooo!" he shouted, sinking into a chair.

"God bless Mr. Publisher's Warehouse," said Mother. She giggled almost the way Poppy did and sat on Daddy's knee. "Are there really two and a half bathrooms in that house?"

Daddy spread the floor plan on the table. It showed where all the rooms in the new house would be. Mother put her finger on a tiny square marked *B.R.* "On the first floor, near the back door. Wonderful for the children."

Fielding put his finger on another B.R. on the second floor. "Never have to wait in line again," he said. "You just run around the house till you find a bathroom nobody's using."

Poppy squeezed between Daddy and

Fielding to look at the floor plan. "What's a family room?"

"An extra living room," said Daddy.

"Why do we need an extra one?" Poppy wanted to know.

Daddy laughed and mussed her hair. "No more stepping over and around people at our house."

"The kitchen's huge," said Mother. "Look, there's even a built-in dishwasher."

Daddy grinned at Poppy and the boys. "You've already got four dishwashers."

"Ugh," said Poppy.

"Double ugh," said Wilding.

"Where's Downers Grove?" asked Forrest.

"West of Chicago," said Mother.

"Hard to get to work from way out there," Daddy said thoughtfully. Then he looked up at the clock. "Holy mackerel, I'm late. I told Sam I'd help him move his old refrigerator and install his new freezer before we go to work. I've got to hurry."

Everyone helped while Daddy changed into

his work clothes. Mother made sandwiches. Wilding washed an apple. Poppy put pickles in a plastic bag. Forrest wrapped up some cookies.

"Hungry," said Chryssie.

"Thirsty," said Daisy.

"Hey, we forgot to eat lunch," said Fielding.

Mother laughed. "I never thought I'd see the day."

Little Woody and the twins and Poppy kissed Daddy goodbye. But Fielding wouldn't.

"Slush," he said, and hit Daddy on the arm.

"Hey," said Daddy. "What's wrong in letting your old Dad know you like him?" But he laughed and socked Fielding back.

"Mush," said Wilding.

"Little kid stuff," said Forrest.

They wouldn't kiss Daddy, either.

Daddy looked from one to the other. "It's about time you two guys started thinking for yourselves," he said. But he grinned and slapped their shoulders and left for Sam's.

While everyone ate hot dogs and applesauce and cookies, they talked about the new house.

"There'll be a bedroom just for us big guys," said Forrest.

"Me, too," said Little Woody.

Everyone laughed at "big guy" Little Woody.

"Where will Mrs. Guschelbauer sleep?" asked Chryssie.

They all turned to stare at her. She put down her spoon and slipped her thumb into her mouth.

Mother leaned around Daisy and took Chryssie's thumb out of her mouth. "Mrs. Guschelbauer is going to stay here, baby. But all of us are moving into a nice new house of our very own."

Chryssie's face puckered. Tears spilled down her cheeks. "I want Mrs. Guschelbauer," she sobbed. "Mrs. Guschelbauer!"

Mother picked her up. "There now, you're all worn out and ready for a nap. There's been too much excitement today.

"The rest of you finish eating and change into play shoes. It's too late to go back to school.

But don't go outside until school's out. I'll write notes to your teachers tomorrow."

The kitchen was quiet. From the front of the house came the sound of Chryssie crying for Mrs. Guschelbauer. Then Daisy joined in. Whatever one twin did, the other did, too.

After a time Fielding said, "How'm I gonna get into town to deliver my papers?"

Wilding said, "I'm sure gonna miss Porpoise Class. I'm almost a two-flipper porpoise now."

Forrest said, "Mrs. Ching's gonna miss me, I bet. I pass out the papers."

Poppy didn't say anything. She was thinking about Rosebud. Once Daddy had said that if they ever had a bigger place, she could have an indoors-outdoors cat.

She glowed inside.

Then suddenly she thought about Tink. If they moved away, she might never see Tink again!

"I'm not hungry," said Poppy. She pushed away her plate, and she didn't even take a cookie.

11

Terrible Jane Ellen

All kinds of things happened in the days that followed.

A picture of the Flower family was in the paper the next morning. There they all were, laughing because the man had said "bellybutton."

"That's me! That's me!" said Forrest.

"Can I take the paper to school to show?" asked Poppy. "Can I?"

Fielding laughed. "Wow, Wi, your ears sure stick out."

"Just washed 'em. Couldn't do a thing with 'em," said Wilding, and everybody groaned.

"Mercy me! Daisy's sucking her thumb,"

said Mother. "See, Daisy? There you are, with your thumb in your mouth."

Daisy looked. "Not me," she said. She wouldn't believe the girl in the picture was really her.

"That's a mighty good-looking family," Daddy said proudly. He smiled at Mother. "And that's one mighty smart lady there."

Mother turned pink.

Poppy read the story aloud: "New Home for a Bunch of Flowers." Everybody groaned.

> Mrs. Barbara Flower, mother of seven, is shown with her family in their apartment at 546 Greenbrier Street. Mrs. Flower submitted the winning entry in a contest held by a magazine subscription company. The family will move out of a small, third-floor apartment into a roomy four-bedroom home to be built for them in a western suburb.

All their names were in the paper. And the story told how Mother made some of their clothes and how she sometimes wrote poems just because she liked to.

The newspaper article made Mother sound like someone Poppy didn't know—a stranger.

But then Mother said, "Fielding, can you get us extra copies to mail to the grandmas and grandpas and cousins? Now everybody, eat your cereal or you'll be late for school."

The lady in the paper seemed strange, but she was the same Mother, after all.

The telephone rang and rang. People called to say congratulations. They even called from as far away as Iowa and Ohio. The phone rang so much Mother set the kitchen timer for five minutes and only talked until the bell rang.

The mailman brought bundles of cards that said "Congratulations" and "Happy Days Are Here." Mother pinned them on a yellow ribbon and hung it next to the refrigerator.

Every day after school Poppy looked at the new cards and counted them. "Twenty," she said. Then, "thirty-five," she said the next day. After a week she counted "sixty-seven!" And there were three yellow ribbons instead of one.

It was a lively, laughing, happy time.

One hot day Poppy was playing with Rosebud in the square of green grass next to the front steps.

Terrible Jane Ellen came out of her house and crossed the street. She was eating an orange Popsicle. She stood kicking at the bottom step, staring at Poppy, taking long licks of the cold, sweet ice.

Poppy untied the yarn doll from the zipper pull on her jacket and dangled it in front of Rosebud. Rosebud pounced and almost caught it. Poppy held the doll higher.

"Dumb cat," said Jane Ellen. She licked the Popsicle again and smacked her lips.

Poppy pretended not to hear. She let Rosebud catch the yarn doll.

Jane Ellen stopped kicking the step. Her green eyes became narrow. "You think you're so smart just because your mother won that house."

"I don't think I'm so smart," Poppy said quietly. But a tight feeling was growing inside her. Jane Ellen was picking a fight.

"Well, my mother says you're all getting big heads just because you hit it lucky," said Jane Ellen. "Who cares if you got your old picture in the newspaper, anyway."

Poppy planted her feet wide and put her hands on her hips. She glared at Jane Ellen. "I think you better go over to your own side of the street, Jane Ellen."

Jane Ellen backed away, still licking her Popsicle. "Mrs. Doppleman says you're all gonna look mighty funny in that fancy new house in your hand-me-down clothes." She turned and ran. As she did, the orange ice fell to the sidewalk, and she was left with just the stick in her hand.

Rosebud ran to the Popsicle. She licked, looked surprised by the coldness, and then ate it eagerly.

"Rosebud's not a dumb cat, Jane Ellen," Poppy yelled. "She's got your Popsicle!"

Jane Ellen stood on the other side of the street, looking disappointed.

Poppy ran indoors. Mother was in the living

room on her knees beside the old green chair. She was making a new cover for it.

Poppy leaned against the sofa, watching her smooth and pin the orange and yellow cloth.

Mother sat back and brushed her hair away from her eyes. "There. Won't that be pretty in our new house?"

"Mom?" asked Poppy. "Are we poor?"

"Poor!" Mother looked at her hard. "Daddy makes a very good living. We have something in the bank. And we just won a new house— remember?"

Poppy drew a circle on the floor with her toe. "Well, why do we buy our clothes at the resale store?"

"You children grow out of things so fast it's foolish to pay what new clothes cost," said Mother. "Daddy and I would rather save the money for big things—like the color TV."

Poppy didn't say anything.

Wilding came into the living room. He turned a chair around, sat on it backwards, and leaned his chin on the back, listening.

"What's the trouble, baby?" Mother asked.

Poppy told about Jane Ellen. "She sounded so mean."

Mother sighed. "Some folks can't stand another person's good luck. They feel hateful and say hateful things."

"Big-mouth Tom Duffy said we were getting stuck-up," said Wilding. "I poked him in the nose."

"Don't fight," said Mother, "or say mean things back. And try not to feel bad. We're going to be happy in our new house."

Poppy started to follow Wilding outdoors.

"Poppy," called Mother. She looked thoughtful. "If wearing things from the resale store is beginning to bother you, why, we'll stop buying your clothes there. I'll just make your things." She smiled. "Life is going to be much easier for us from now on."

Poppy went outdoors feeling good about Mother's promise. But—she couldn't help it—she still hurt at the thought of Jane Ellen's meanness.

That night Poppy woke up. The street light shining through the trees made moving shadows on the wall. She watched sleepily. The shadows had shapes—a ball, a horse's head, a face. Tink's face!

Tink. Poppy sat up. Maybe she was going to move away and never, ever see Tink again.

Suddenly Poppy didn't want to be alone. She slid out of her bunk bed and pattered out of the bedroom.

The dining room was dark, but there was a light in the kitchen. Mother and Daddy were sitting at the table. Daddy was adding numbers on a piece of paper and talking about "the terrible taxes" and getting to work "from way out there."

Poppy leaned sleepily against the dining-room table, blinking at the light from the kitchen.

Mother said something about "an upsetting time for the kids." She put her hand on Daddy's arm. "It's been a good life right here on Greenbrier Street," she said. Then she saw Poppy.

"Mercy, Poppy," she said. "What on earth are you doing out of bed at this hour?"

"Want a drink," said Poppy, although she wasn't at all sure that's what she wanted. It was just nicer to be in the lighted kitchen with Mother and Daddy than it was to be watching shadows on the bedroom wall and thinking about leaving Tink.

Daddy pushed back his chair and patted his knee. "Is my Number One Daughter too grown-up to sit on her old Daddy's lap?"

Poppy was pretty old. But all the same, that sounded like a very nice idea. She slid onto his lap and snuggled against him.

Mother turned on the radio, and soft music filled the kitchen. Then she heated some milk and gave it to Poppy in one of the pretty yellow mugs she saved for company.

Poppy took a sip.

"Tink," she said. "I'll never see Tink again." Her voice wobbled.

Mother and Daddy looked at each other over Poppy's head.

"You'll visit Tink after we move," said Daddy. "I promise."

"Tink can come to see us. She can stay overnight," said Mother.

Poppy felt better. She drank her milk while Daddy smoothed her hair and patted her arm. Then he and Mother talked about "Spring and Cheryl and the kids" and "that time before we were married" and "someday we'll all go to Disneyland."

Poppy yawned. It felt cozy to be all alone with Mother and Daddy . . . almost in the middle of the night . . . sitting on Daddy's lap . . . with his hand going pat-pat-pat on her arm . . . listening to grown-up talk . . .

Her eyes closed.

When she opened them it was morning. She was back in bed, and she didn't remember how she got there.

12

Best Friends

After that, Terrible Jane Ellen stayed on her own side of the street. All she did was stick out her tongue sometimes.

The days grew warm. School ended, and Poppy passed into the next grade. She felt grown-up and glad, but she knew she was going to miss Mrs. Robbin. It isn't every day you have a teacher with a bird's name!

Poppy and Tink spent all their days together, for soon Poppy would move away to the new house and then when would they see each other?

They signed up for summer craft classes, swam at the park pool, drew pictures, tried to learn to ride Wilding's skateboard, went fishing early one morning and caught a fish for Rosebud.

But the best thing was—

"Can you sleep at my house tonight?" Tink asked one Saturday.

They went to find Poppy's mother.

"We're going to send out for food," Tink said.

"Well . . . "

"We'll go to bed early," Tink promised.

"If—" said Mother.

"And my mother's staying home tonight!" said Tink.

Mother smiled. "What a good time you'll have!" she said.

So while Mother called Tink's mother to be sure everything was all right, Poppy packed her nightie and comb and toothbrush. And then she went home with Tink.

Tink's house was very different from Poppy's. The carpet in the living room was apple red. The sheer curtains were pale gray. Golden holders on the wall held red candles.

And Tink's mother, Mrs. Becker, was as different from Poppy's mother as could be. Her blond hair curled around her face and hung around her shoulders. She put on lipstick and eye makeup even when nobody was around. She wore high, high heels, even with her jeans.

"Your mother's just like a TV star," Poppy whispered when they went to the kitchen for Cokes.

"She has to look nice," said Tink. "She says the ladies at the beauty shop expect her to."

They carried the Cokes to the living room. Tink's mother was curled up on the sofa painting her long fingernails with shiny red polish. They looked gorgeous. She reached for a Coke. She moved her hand carefully, holding her fingers out so the nail polish wouldn't smear.

Tink turned on the TV and they started to watch a movie.

"Whoops!" said Tink's mother. "I nearly forgot. I bought a chocolate cake. Wouldn't that be good with this Coke!"

Tink and Poppy went back to the kitchen. Mrs. Becker's voice followed them. "Tinkerbell . . . use the company dishes."

Tink giggled. She climbed on a chair and found some flowered paper plates. "Our best company dishes," she said. Poppy giggled, too.

They cut the cake and took the plates back to the living room, licking chocolate frosting off their fingers.

"Yummy!" Mrs. Becker laughed. "Poppy, we always have dessert before dinner."

Was there anything nicer than dessert before dinner? Tink's mother didn't act like a mother at all!

They watched the movie, an old one.

"Wow!" Tink exclaimed. "Look at those clothes! Do you suppose the ladies in those days thought they looked *pretty*?" The dresses were floppy and long. With them, the stars wore rolled-down ankle socks and high-heeled shoes.

"Do you suppose they ever wore jeans?" Poppy wondered.

Even Mrs. Becker, who was old, didn't know the answer to that. "Will you look at that one's hair. It's so stiff! I'll bet if she fell down it would break! Of course," she added, "our hair-dressing aids weren't invented then."

Still, the movie was fun. It was a musical and there were dance numbers with long lines of tap dancers tapping away, their arms swinging loosely at their sides.

At the very best part, just when the pretty young girl was going to have her big chance to sing and dance on stage, the doorbell chimed.

"That must be the pizza," said Tink's mother. "Run down and get it, Tink. The money's on the dining-room table."

Tink didn't take her eyes off the TV. "I want to see what happens next."

"I'll tell you what happens," said her mother. "Run, before the delivery man thinks we're not home."

"Uh-uh," said Tink. "You go."

Poppy listened, round-eyed. Was Tink's mother going to get angry?

Mrs. Becker pushed herself to her feet. "Honestly, you are the absolute end, Tink." Looking over her shoulder at the TV, she trailed out of the room.

Poppy couldn't believe it. The way they argued, Tink and her mother sounded just like two little girls!

Poppy went back to watching the movie. The young girl sang and danced. The people clapped and clapped, and she bowed again and again.

Mrs. Becker came back with the pizza. "What happened?"

Tink sighed happily. "She's going to be a star."

"I missed it," Mrs. Becker said sadly. She cut the pizza and gave big pieces to the girls on fresh paper plates. "Well, maybe I'll see it again on the late show."

They ate hungrily and washed the pizza down with Coke. Then they had more Coke and more chocolate cake. It was the best supper Poppy ever ate.

Tink's mother made a face at the mess on the coffee table. "Dear me," she said in a proper-lady voice, "it's time to do the dishes. Shall we show Poppy how we do dishes, Tink?"

Tink grinned. She gathered up her plate and napkin and followed her mother to the kitchen. Mrs. Becker did a perky dance step, and Tink did exactly the same step.

Her nose in the air, Tink's mother looked down at Tink. "How do we do dishes?" she asked in her proper-lady voice.

"This is how we do dishes." Tink spoke in a proper-lady voice, too. She held her plate high above the wastebasket and let go. It fluttered into the trash. Her mother laughed and did the same thing.

Poppy tossed away her plate as happily as Tink had. Imagine never having to wash dishes!

Halfway through a cowboy movie, the phone rang. Tink's mother answered it. "Hello? . . . Watching an old movie with Tink and her friend . . . well, I don't know—I told Tink I'd stay home . . . "

Tink's head turned.

" . . . maybe later, then . . . for a while."

"You promised you'd stay home," Tink whispered loudly.

Her mother waved her hand for Tink to be quiet.

"Well, all right. Eleven o'clock." She hung up.

"You promised," Tink yelled.

"Now, Tinkerbell, don't act up," said her mother.

"I'm not acting up," yelled Tink.

"Really, what difference does it make?" asked her mother. "I'll be here the whole evening. You'll be in bed and asleep when I leave."

It sounded right. But somehow it wasn't right at all. Tink's face was red, and there were tears in her eyes.

Poppy and Tink finished watching the movie, took a bubble bath, brushed their teeth.

The red faded from Tink's face, but she didn't smile a lot.

Her mother told jokes and showed them how to do an old-fashioned dance called a buck-and-wing.

Tink smiled.

Her mother held a comb the way singers

hold microphones and sang a silly song, and Tink laughed aloud. Poppy felt better, too, glad Tink was back to her usual happy self.

They all ate more chocolate cake and drank more Coke.

"Now you'll have to brush your teeth again," said Tink's mother. "You want to have pretty teeth when you grow up, don't you?"

At last Mrs. Becker helped them into bed, but first she had to clear away Tink's eleven stuffed animals.

"I'll leave the bedroom door open," she said, "and the living-room light on. Now you settle down and go to sleep."

"Will you let us see you in your dress-up clothes?" asked Tink. "Before you go out?"

Her mother promised. "If you're still awake, that is . . ."

They meant to stay awake. They tried.

"When I grow up," whispered Poppy, "I'm going to live in a house right next door to yours."

"When I grow up," whispered Tink, "I'll let

my daughter's best friend sleep over every night if she wants to."

"We'll still be best friends," whispered Poppy. She yawned.

"We'll have daughters and they'll be best friends, too," whispered Tink.

"Our granddaughters, too," said Poppy. What a funny idea!

"And our great granddaughters," said Tink, "and our great-great-granddaughters . . ."

And they fell asleep.

Poppy woke up first. At the foot of the bed were two fuzzy, yellow ducks. One wore a green cowboy hat, the other an orange one.

"Tink," Poppy whispered.

Sleepily Tink opened her eyes.

Poppy pointed. "Look."

Tink yawned and stretched. Then she crawled to the end of the bed and got the ducks. She gave the one with the green hat to Poppy. "This one's for you," she said, and, "My mom just loves to surprise me. Now I've got twelve stuffed animals!"

13

Another Surprise

Mother and Daddy talked about the new house a lot. They went downtown to see the people from Publishers' Warehouse. They went other places, too, but they didn't tell Poppy and the boys where they went.

One Saturday morning Daddy came home from work and didn't go to bed. Instead, he took the twins and Little Woody to Mrs. Guschelbauer's. Then he and Mother got dressed up and went away.

For some reason Poppy felt the way she did before Christmas—excited and watchful. The boys felt that way, too. Nobody went far from home.

Forrest sat on the steps with his friends Mark and Tim, looking at comic books.

Wilding and Matt hung around Matt's

house, across the street, riding their skateboards.

Fielding rode his bike up and down the block. He rode no-hands and did wheelies and other hard tricks nobody else could do.

Tink had a brand-new piece of pink chalk. She made hopscotch squares on the sidewalk, and she and Poppy played in front of Poppy's house. Rosebud played with them, pouncing on the stone they tossed into the squares.

Tink had to go home for lunch before Poppy saw Mother and Daddy come up the street. She ran to meet them.

They weren't carrying bags of groceries. "You didn't go shopping," Poppy said.

Mother smiled at Daddy as though they shared a secret. "Well, in a way we did go shopping," she said. "Come inside, everyone, and we'll tell you about it."

Mother and Daddy went into the house, and everyone trooped after them.

They knocked on Mrs. Guschelbauer's door. Little Woody and the twins tumbled out to meet them. Daddy lifted Little Woody to his shoulders, and they all went upstairs together.

Mother sat down at the kitchen table and looked around at them.

"Now?" asked Daddy.

"Now," Mother said quietly.

"Well," said Daddy, "Mom and I have been thinking about moving way out there to the suburbs. It's pretty far from town, and I need to be near my job."

"And Greenbrier Street is such a nice place to live," said Mother.

"So we decided not to take that new house," said Daddy. "We took the money instead."

Mother's eyes danced. "We just went down to the next block. There's a house for sale there that we like. We're buying that one instead of moving to the house I won."

The only sound in the kitchen came from the water dripping in the sink.

"We're not going to move away from Greenbrier Street," Mother said into the stillness.

Happy sounds exploded in the kitchen.

"Tink and I can still be best friends," said Poppy.

"I can stay in Porpoise Class," said Wilding.

"We can go back to Armbruster in the fall," said Forrest.

"I can keep my paper route," said Fielding.

"Right," laughed Daddy. "Everybody's right. And we'll have a big-enough house, too. The place is old, but it's interesting. And it has plenty of space."

"The rooms are sunny," said Mother. "There's a fireplace in the living room and lots of bedrooms and two bathrooms."

"Can Rosebud come to live with us?" asked Poppy.

"Oh, I'd say there'll be room for a cat," said Daddy. "Wouldn't you, Mother?"

"How about some white mice?" asked Forrest.

"And a rabbit?" asked Wilding. "For my magic act."

"And a little blue bird that talks?" asked Chryssie.

"And a yellow bird that sings?" asked Daisy.

"Gotta have a dog, too," said Fielding.

"Doggie?" asked Little Woody. "Doggie?"

Everybody turned to stare at him.

"Ma!" said Fielding. "Woody talked! He said something!"

"Woody's our big boy," said Mother, lifting him into her lap. "Say it again, Woody. Say *doggie.*"

Everybody waited.

"Me, too," said Little Woody. "Me, too!"

14

The Happiest Day

It was going to be the happiest day of Poppy's whole life. The Flowers were moving into their wonderful new-old house.

Uncle Spring and Uncle Dennis came in a U-Drive truck, and Daddy's friend Sam came with his tool box to help fix things in the new place. Poppy and Tink and the boys climbed in and out of the truck with each piece of furniture the men brought downstairs.

At last Daddy said he didn't need any more extra help. "Why don't you kids run down to the new house and look things over," he said. He gave the key to Fielding. "You're in charge." He looked around at everyone. "Hear that?"

It was spooky-fun to go into the new house without any grown-ups. Poppy held Rosebud close, and Tink stayed right beside her. Their footsteps echoed in the empty rooms.

Poppy led the way into the living room to show Tink the fireplace. Rosebud leaped up onto the fireplace mantel. There, another gray cat looked back at her from the mirror.

Rosebud looked surprised. Her fur stood out. Her back humped. She hissed and jumped back down.

Poppy and Tink laughed.

"This is where we'll hang our stockings at Christmas," said Poppy.

"You can hang a little one for Rosebud, too," said Tink.

Rosebud had gone back into the front hall. Poppy and Tink found her scratching at the door.

Poppy gathered her up and showed her the window seat next to the door. "You can wait here for me to come home from school every day, Rosebud. I'll see you when I come up the steps."

Under the curving stairway that led to the second floor, a door opened into a small room. It was lined with bookshelves.

"Imagine having enough books to fill all these shelves," said Poppy.

"Didn't the people who used to live here know about the public library?" Tink asked.

Tink opened another door in the hall. Behind it, only inches away, was—another wall! Dozens of small hooks covered it.

Poppy was puzzled. "I wonder what this is for," she said.

Fielding came into the hall just then. "That's a key closet. Mom told me about it."

"Why do you need a closet for keys?" asked Tink.

"There's a hook for every key in this house," Fielding explained. "That way the keys never get lost. It's the way people did things in the olden days."

Was there a house anywhere else in the world that had a closet for keys?

Wilding and Forrest raced through the hall. Poppy, holding Rosebud, and Tink followed them through the dining room and pantry and into the kitchen.

Wilding opened a small door high on one wall. Inside was a kind of box with ropes on it. He pulled a rope, and the box moved upward.

"That's a dumbwaiter," Fielding said importantly. "When rich people used to live here a long time ago, the servants sent things upstairs and down in it."

Wilding's happy-go-lucky grin showed. "A guy could fit into this."

"Oh, no you don't," said Fielding.

"Who says?" asked Wilding.

"I says," said Fielding. "I'm the oldest and in charge, and you know doggone well we'll both be in trouble if you try to ride in that dumb-waiter."

Wilding looked grumpy. But he didn't climb into the box.

Upstairs, Poppy showed Tink the room Mother had said was to be hers, hers alone. It was smaller than the other bedrooms, but exactly right for one person. The roof slanted in one corner, and tiny windows looked out over the street. Poppy closed the door so Rosebud wouldn't get away again, and they stayed there, watching the men bring in furniture from the truck.

Overhead came the sound of the boys running and sliding in the big room Mother said had once been a ballroom.

"You mean like the kind in 'Cinderella?'" Poppy had asked.

"Not as big as in a castle," Mother had explained. "When our house was built, people called a party a *ball*, and many people had big rooms just for those parties. They called them ballrooms."

The boys were making a terrible racket up there.

Moving day came to an end at last. All of the furniture, all of the boxes, all of the curtains had been brought to the new house.

The uncles drove away in the empty truck.

Sam left his tool box. "Those front-porch steps need work," he said to Daddy. "I'll come next week to give you a hand with them."

Tink went home. She didn't really want to go. "But my mom will be home from work any minute," she said.

Poppy, holding Rosebud, waved to her from the front door. Rosebud squirmed and jumped out of Poppy's arms. Just in time Poppy shut the door, or Rosebud would have slipped through. She nosed at the crack. Then she turned and trotted into the living room. Poppy followed her.

Daddy was lying on the sofa. Little Woody was sitting on his chest.

The room looked almost like home. Near the fireplace stood the old green chair in its bright, new orange and yellow cover, its own special spot of sunshine.

Mother came into the living room. "Imagine! Mrs. Guschelbauer brought over two hot dishes for supper. That dear woman!"

She dropped into a chair. "Here we all are, moved into our big new house. Isn't this the happiest day!"

Rosebud walked to the middle of the room. She sniffed the air and stretched slowly. Then, lazily, she went to the orange and yellow chair. She stood up, her front paws on the chair.

"Poppy," said Mother, "get the cat before she—"

Zii-ii-iip! The harsh sound of ripping cloth filled the room.

"Ohhhhhh," sighed Mother.

Poppy's mouth opened. She couldn't move. She could only stare at the long rip in the pretty new chair cover. What would Mother say! Poppy looked at her.

Mother's eyes were full of tears. She was going to cry!

Mothers weren't supposed to cry, especially not on the happiest day.

"That does it," Daddy said firmly, "that—"

Poppy didn't let him finish. "I guess maybe Rosebud doesn't want to be an indoors cat. She's been trying to get away all day." She swallowed. "Come on, Rosie-bud. You can go outside if you want to."

Her head high, Rosebud trotted out of the living room.

Through the hall.

Out the door that Poppy held open for her.

Down the steps.

And up the street, toward the old house, and her own little house under the back steps.

Poppy watched her go. But she didn't watch very well, for it's hard to see through tears.

And that was not the happiest day of Poppy's whole life, after all.

15

Any Old Kind of Cat

Poppy sat on the steps. She hugged her knees and pressed her wet face against them. "I guess Rosie-bud doesn't like me," she thought. "If she did, she would want to stay here in our new house and be my indoors cat."

She knew she was never going to be happy again.

After a while the screen door squeaked. Footsteps stopped beside her.

Poppy didn't look up.

"Please don't feel bad, Poppy," whispered Chryssie.

Poppy felt a wet kiss on her cheek.

"You take Muffer for a while," whispered Daisy.

"And here's Teddy Eddie, too," whispered Chryssie.

Poppy felt the two old stuffed animals, the dearest things the twins owned, being pushed into her lap.

"You can keep Muffer till I have to go to sleep," said Daisy.

"You can hold Teddy Eddie all you want, even tomorrow," said Chryssie.

The little girls sat down on the steps and didn't talk. Now and then one of them patted Poppy's knee.

Soon the screen door opened and banged shut.

"Popp, here's my best comic books." It was Forrest. "You can look at 'em tonight."

The comic books made a slapping sound as Forrest put them down on the step.

Poppy swallowed. "Thanks, Forr," she whispered, touching the rumpled pages.

The screen door banged again.

Fielding pushed several round, hard, flat things into Poppy's hand. "Go get a Thirty-One Flavors, Popp," he said. "Get any kind you want."

Fielding was giving her money! Fielding never gave away his money. Nobody could even find out where he hid it!

Poppy sniffed. She wiped her wet eyes on Muffer. "Gee, thanks, Fee," she whispered. "That's pretty neat."

But would she ever want another Thirty-One Flavors ice-cream cone? Poppy didn't think so.

Wilding came outside next. He pushed a handful of new cards under her chin. "Take a card, Popp," he said. "Any card."

Poppy didn't feel like taking a card, any card.

"Aw, come on, Popp," said Wilding. "Don't be like that."

So Poppy took a card.

"Don't tell me," said Wilding. "I, the great Wilding the Magnificent, say it is . . . it is . . ." He closed his eyes. He put his hand to his forehead. "Is it—uh, I mean, it *is* the eight of clubs."

Poppy looked. It was! Wilding had learned

how to do the card trick! "Wi! You did it! Wow!"

Wilding beamed.

Poppy hugged Muffer and Teddy Eddie. It was nice to have sisters and brothers gather around when you felt absolutely terrible and sad. And she never even remembered that once—a long time ago—she had wished she was an only child.

The screen door opened and closed once more.

Daddy came and sat down on one side of her. Mother sat down on the other side.

"Feeling kind of bad, huh, Sis?" asked Daddy.

Poppy nodded.

"Poppy," said Mother, "I can patch the chair cover. The rip will hardly show. We'll put the table next to it."

"I didn't think Rosebud would do that," whispered Poppy.

"I know you didn't," said Mother.

Poppy smoothed Teddy Eddie's rough fur.

"I wanted Rosebud to live with me in our new house," she went on. "I wanted her to be my indoors cat, the way Daddy promised."

Daddy coughed. "Well, uh, I don't know that I exactly promised. But it looks like she isn't an indoors kind of cat," he said.

"Hey, Popp," said Wilding. "Remember when you found her? You said you were gonna help her be the best outdoors cat that ever was."

"Is that what you said, Poppy?" asked Mother. "Is that what you did?"

Poppy lifted her head. "I guess she always finds something to eat," she said proudly. "I helped her learn to do that."

"You helped her to be free and to survive," said Daddy. "That was a good thing to do."

"But now that she's free," said Mother, "she doesn't need a house. She can't change, now, and be cooped up. Now she has to stay free."

"You can be proud you did such a good job, Sis," said Daddy.

It was true. She had done a good job. For a moment Poppy felt better.

Then she thought how much she wanted Rosebud to stay and how much Rosebud had wanted to get away. She swallowed. "If Rosebud liked me enough, she would want to stay and be my indoors cat. She doesn't like me enough."

Everyone on the porch steps was quiet.

Mother spoke at last. "Rosebud does like you. If she didn't, she would have been off and away long, long ago."

Poppy didn't say anything.

"But she stayed nearby," said Mother. "All the things you did, she seemed to like. She liked you just the way you are, baby."

Poppy rubbed Teddy Eddie's one black eye.

Mother went on. "You're going to have to learn to say, 'Rosebud, you can still be my outdoors cat. I'll love you anyway. You can come and go as you please.'"

"You do that, Sis," said Daddy, "and you'll feel better."

Mother kissed her.

Daddy patted her hair.

And then everybody went indoors.

Poppy hugged floppy old Muffer and limp old Teddy Eddie.

She touched the coins in her pocket.

The wind ruffled the pages of the comic books.

Behind her in the house the boys were playing something noisy on the stairs.

Suddenly a quiet gray shadow came around the corner of the house.

Poppy caught her breath.

Rosebud sat on the path in the sun. She yawned. She scratched her ear with her right hind foot. She watched a bug for a long time, then placed a paw on it.

Slowly, walking like a queen, she came to the steps and wound herself around Poppy's ankles. She sat on the step, her tail in a tidy circle around her feet.

Poppy touched her. She could feel Rosebud purring.

"Hey, Popp," Wilding called. "Ma says come in. We're all putting our own stuff away."

Poppy talked to Rosebud. "I found you. I gave you a name. I helped you learn to be an outdoors cat. I guess—"

"Hurry up, Popp," called Forrest. "We're waiting for you."

"—I guess you don't have to be an indoors cat," said Poppy. "I just guess you can be any old kind of cat you want to be."

There! She had said the hard words.

The next part was easier. "I like you whatever way you are, Rosie-bud."

Rosebud turned and looked right up at Poppy, almost as though she understood exactly what Poppy was saying.

Poppy got up. She went to the door.

Rosebud followed. But she sat down when the door opened. She wouldn't go in.

Poppy looked back through the screen. "Okay, Rosie-bud," she said. "Okay."

What Happened Later

And so Rosebud never became an indoors cat. She remained an outdoors cat who came and went as she pleased. But she and Poppy were friends.

She let Poppy hold her—the only person who could do that. She purred when Poppy petted her. And when she had kittens, in the box under the steps behind the old house, Poppy was the only person who could touch them.

One warm summer day Poppy and Tink were sitting in the tree in Poppy's backyard. Poppy was reading a book. Tink was drawing a picture.

Tink looked down through the leaves. "Look. Here comes Rosebud. What's she got?"

Poppy peeked through the leaves. "She's caught something again." She sighed. "I hope it's not a bird." She tucked her book into the back of her jeans and slid down the tree.

126

Tink followed. "Hey," she breathed when she saw what Rosebud was carrying.

Rosebud set a small bundle of fur at Poppy's feet.

"Nice cat, Rosie-bud," said Poppy. "Good cat!" And this time she really meant those words. Rosebud was bringing one of the kittens to her!

Rosebud sat back to rest.

Poppy held the kitten against her cheek until it wiggled. Then she put it on the grass.

The kitten went to its mother on wobbly legs and pushed against her. But Rosebud wouldn't let it feed. Instead, she got up and trotted out of the yard.

The kitten tried to follow her. But it couldn't move fast enough. It sat down, crying sad little squeaks and mews. Then it saw a beetle. It forgot its mother and followed the beetle with its nose.

"Why do you suppose Rosebud brought it here?" asked Tink.

A shiny bubble of an idea began to grow in

Poppy's mind. She sat back on her heels. "I think she brought the kitten because it isn't safe under the steps anymore."

Gently Tink touched the kitten. "That's true. There's that big brown dog around there now."

The bubble of an idea grew bigger. "Rosebud's going to come back here any old minute with the other kitten." Poppy was sure of it. "She knows they will be safe here."

Tink's eyes were like saucers. "Poppy! You'll have two kittens!"

Poppy laughed and shook her head. "No, I won't," she said, cuddling the kitten. "I'll have one and you'll have one. We'll each have a kitten, and we'll teach them to be the best indoors cats that ever were."

And *that* was the happiest day of Poppy's whole life.